HELEN LESTER

The Wizard
the Fairy and
the Magic Chicken

Illustrated by LYNN MUNSINGER

Houghton Mifflin Company Boston

Library of Congress Cataloging in Publication Data

Lester, Helen.
   The wizard, the fairy, and the magic chicken.

   Summary: When three boastful magicians try to outdo
one another, they create a problem that can be solved
only when they work together.
   [1. Magic—Fiction. 2. Friendship—Fiction]
I. Munsinger, Lynn, ill. II. Title.
PZ7.L56285Wi   1983   [E]   82-21302

Printed in the United States of America

RNF   ISBN   0-395-33885-9
PAP   ISBN   0-395-47945-2

RNF   H   &   PAP   N   10 9 8 7 6 5 4 3

There once lived a Wizard, a Fairy, and a Magic Chicken.
Each thought, "I am the greatest in the world."
And each was very jealous of the other two.

"MY wand has a MOON on it," said the Wizard.

"MY wand has a STAR on it," said the Fairy.

"MY wand has a PICKLE on it,"
   said the Magic Chicken.

"I can kiss a pig

and turn it into a bicycle," said the Wizard.

"That's nothing," said the Fairy.   "I can kiss a bicycle
and turn it into a bowl of soup."

"I can do better than that,"
said the Magic Chicken.
"I can kiss a bowl of soup
and turn it into a singing frog."

Each one always tried to outdo the others.

"I can make a hairy
monster with sharp teeth!"
bellowed the Wizard.

"I can make a bumpy monster with nine legs!"
screeched the Fairy.

"I can make a dotted monster with buggy eyes!"
yelled the Magic Chicken.

The monsters glared at the magicians and loudly said,
"GRRRRRRROLPH!"

For the very first time the magicians agreed.

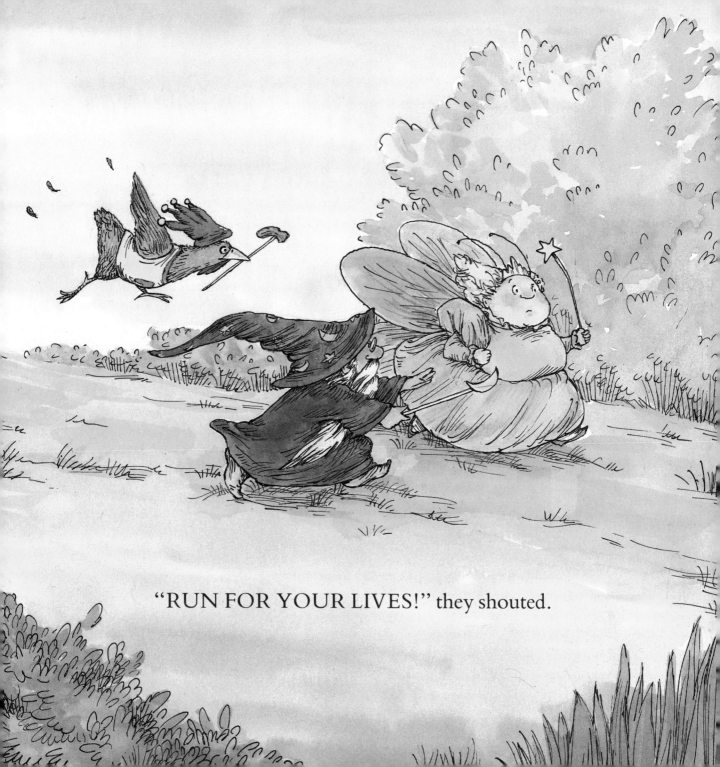

"RUN FOR YOUR LIVES!" they shouted.

"I will make a cloud to hide behind," gasped the Wizard,
but that didn't stop the monsters.

"I will make thunder to scare them," puffed the Fairy,
but the monsters were not frightened.

"I will make lightning. That will make them go away,"
cried the Magic Chicken, but they would not go away.
Nothing worked.

"We'd better . . ." said the Wizard.

". . . try something . . ." said the Fairy.

". . . together!" said the Magic Chicken.

So they chanted, "One, two, three, GO!"
The cloud and the thunder and the lightning came together.
Suddenly it rained.

It rained so hard and the monsters got so wet that they shrank
until they were only very little monsters and
not scary at all.
"We did it!" cheered the Wizard, the Fairy, and the Magic Chicken.
"I must say, though," said the Wizard, "my cloud made the rain."
"Well," said the Fairy, "it was because of my thunder."
"But not without my lightning," said the Magic Chicken.

There once lived a Wizard, a Fairy, and a Magic Chicken.
They argued a lot,
but deep down they were very good friends.